KU-183-263

Go to Sleep or I
LET LOOSE
the LEOPARD

Steve Cole
Bruce Ingman

JONATHAN CAPE · LONDON

TOWER HAMLETS LIBRARIES	
91000004544516	
Bertrams	09/12/2014
	£6.99
THCUB	TH14001588

It was Joe and Ellie's bedtime.

But Joe and Ellie
were **not** in bed.

They were fighting mattress-monsters,
catching creatures with the curtains. . .
They were wrestling wild wardrobes!

BOUNCE. ZAPP!
Yee-HOOOO. **BANG.**

TOWER HAMLETS

91 000 004 544 51 6

Go to Sleep or I
LET LOOSE
the LEOPARD

idea
Library Learning Information

To renew this item call:
0115 929 3388
or visit
www.ideastore.co.uk

TOWER HAMLETS

Created and managed by Tower Hamlets Council

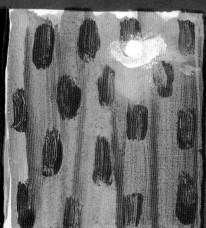

For Amy, ever and always – S.C.

For my real life go-to-bed monkeys,
Alvie and Ted – B.I.

GO TO SLEEP OR I LET LOOSE THE LEOPARD
A JONATHAN CAPE BOOK 978 1 780 08062 8
Published in Great Britain by Jonathan Cape, an imprint of Random House Children's Publishers UK A Random House Group Company
This edition published 2014
1 3 5 7 9 10 8 6 4 2
Text copyright © Steve Cole, 2014   Illustrations copyright © Bruce Ingman, 2014
The right of Steve Cole and Bruce Ingman to be identified as the author and illustrator of this work has been asserted in accordance with the Copyright, Designs and Patents Act 1988.
All rights reserved. No part of this publication may be reproduced, stored in a retrieval system, or transmitted in any form or by any means, electronic, mechanical, photocopying,
recording or otherwise, without the prior permission of the publishers. RANDOM HOUSE CHILDREN'S PUBLISHERS UK 61–63 Uxbridge Road, London W5 5SA
www.randomhousechildrens.co.uk www.randomhouse.co.uk
Addresses for companies within The Random House Group Limited can be found at: www.randomhouse.co.uk/offices.htm
THE RANDOM HOUSE GROUP Limited Reg. No. 954009
A CIP catalogue record for this book is available from the British Library.
Printed in China

FSC
www.fsc.org
MIX
Paper from
responsible sources
FSC® C104723

The Random House Group Limited supports the Forest Stewardship Council® (FSC®), the leading international forest-certification organisation. Our books carrying the FSC label are printed on FSC®-certified paper.
FSC is the only forest-certification scheme supported by the leading environmental organisations, including Greenpeace. Our paper procurement policy can be found at www.randomhouse.co.uk/environment

The New Babysitter
had to come upstairs.

For the
twenty-seventh
time!

(She had been telling
them off all night.)
"**You** are testing my
patience," she said.
"If you do not go to bed **NOW**
you will be very, **_very_** sorry!"

"**OK.**" Joe and Ellie nodded
and plodded back to bed.

And the New Babysitter
went downstairs again.
The house was quiet.

For a whole
TEN SECONDS.

Joe and Ellie were up again.

They were sailing in the bookcase,
braving **Pirate Chief Pyjamas.**

They were caught
in carpet whirlpools –

SLOOSH.

Ah-HARRR.

WHOOOSH.

AiiEEEEEEE!

The New Babysitter stomped back upstairs
for the ***twenty-eighth*** time.

"I warned you!"

She began to rumble like a rocket ready to rise.

"If you two are not asleep in **THIRTY SECONDS,**

I will put your whole room in a spaceship

and send you to the **moon!**"

"No you won't!"
laughed Joe.
"Our room
would **never**
fit in a spaceship.
You don't even
HAVE
a spaceship."

"I have a better idea," said the New Babysitter.

"If you two are not asleep in

TWENTY SECONDS,

I will fetch my special robot

who will **zap** you with a sleep ray!"

"You haven't ***got*** a robot,"
giggled Ellie.
"And even if you did,
it couldn't get **US!**"

"I have an even better idea,"
said the New Babysitter.
"Bed in **TEN** seconds, or I'll fetch
a **toy-munching monster**
to babysit you instead."

"**There's no such thing,**"
scoffed Joe.

"Bed in **FIVE** seconds or I'll put a **naughty-child-nibbling plant** from the Jumbalumba Jungle in your room!"

"There's no such place!" laughed Ellie.

And then the New Babysitter
threw her hands above
her head and shouted:

"Go to sleep – or I let loose the LEOPARD!"

Joe and Ellie roared
with laughter.
"You haven't
got a leopard!"

"That's what **_you_** think,"
said the New Babysitter.

She turned calmly.
She left the room calmly.
She went downstairs.
Very, **very** calmly.

And Joe and Ellie stopped laughing.

They heard
the **clunk** of
a key in a lock...
the **squeak**
of a cage door
swinging open...
a **long, low**
GROWL ...

And the **THUMP**
of the New Babysitter's
feet on the stairs as
she ran to their room
and said,
"There...
I ***have***
let loose
the leopard!"

Then Joe and Ellie caught a flash of **yellow** and **black**.

They heard another ***GROWL***.

It was **louder**. It was **closer**.

"You couldn't have."

"You wouldn't have."

"I probably *shouldn't* have."

"But I did."

"So, right *now*, straight away, this **instant**, TOUT DE SUITE, this *very* moment, on the double, on the **TRIPLE**, this precise, exact *nano-second*, please, please, please, please, **PLEASE:** *Go to sleep* –

because . . .

The leopard is **HERE!"**

"And the leopard . . . is **nice!**"

"There!"

The New Babysitter smiled.

"You didn't think I'd let loose
a *nasty* leopard, did you?"

But Joe and Ellie didn't answer.

They were fast asleep at last.

Puff.

Snore.

Snooze.

Flutter.

And not another word was heard from them
all night long.

"**I'm sorry, everyone** –
I won't need you
tonight after all.

The trick with the
leopard actually **worked** . . ."